Jocko the RAVEN

ISBN 978-1-64492-475-4 (paperback)
ISBN 978-1-64492-476-1 (digital)

Christian Faith Publishing, Inc.
832 Park Avenue
Meadville, PA 16335
www.christianfaithpublishing.com

Printed in the United States of America

Jocko the RAVEN

Phil Ellsworth, DVM

Jocko the Raven was just a young bird flying high over the fields and houses of this small town. Of course, he didn't really have a name then, at least the kind that humans use. That came later. One day, Jocko saw someone pointing what looked like a stick at him while he glided in the air currents and then suddenly felt a sting in his wing, and that wing wouldn't work anymore. He started falling toward the ground. He hit the ground rather hard and was knocked out. A young mother and her two children saw the raven spiraling down out of the sky and land beside a small creek. They went to find him as quickly as possible, and the mother wrapped him in her jacket. They decided it's best to take the raven to a veterinarian to see how badly he was hurt.

By the time they got the raven to the vet, he was awake and would struggle to move. The vet examined him, taking an X-ray of the wing and finding that he had been shot with a pellet gun that broke a wing bone. The vet would have to keep him to remove the pellet and set the wing bone. He would have to have his wing wrapped and stay in a cage for some time. That is when he got the name Jocko.

Jocko was fed by the hospital staff twice a day like the other animals. Fortunately, ravens eat lots of different kinds of food, so he ate cat food, dog food, and sometimes some bits of lunch from the hospital staff. He was close to all the things going on in the hospital, and people would talk to him as they went by or when cleaning his cage. One day, he surprised a technician when she went by. And he said, "Hello there," which was a common greeting when he was fed.

She said, "Jocko, what did you say?" And he said, "Hello there," again.

The staff then began repeating more phrases and found that Jocko would pick them up quickly. The veterinarian surmised that the bump on the head that knocked him out briefly had affected his brain and allowed him to learn faster. Doc said that ravens were naturally smart, but Jocko seemed to be extra smart. Jocko was in an area that enabled him to hear conversations and soon learned the names of the technicians and other staff. He would say, "Hi, Judy." or "Hi, Sam." or "Hi, Mary." or "Hi, Doc."

After some weeks, his wing wrap was removed, and he was transferred to a covered run in the kennel area where he could exercise his wings. A couple of narrow boards were placed across the run so he could perch well off of the ground. Sam, the kennel man, also found that Jocko liked the harder food that was fed to the dogs in the runs. He would pick up the pieces and drop them in the water dish to soften them before eating. Pretty smart.

This is where Jocko begins to tell his own story:

I thought it was really fun to see the reactions of the people in the hospital when I began to say their names. I also began to understand some of the things they talked about like "That new puppy is really sick" or "It's time to feed" or "It is time to go home." I didn't understand all of this right away; but as time went on, I could understand what they meant.

I was glad to get the bandage off of my wing. It felt good to be able to stretch it out and move it again. After I had been in this larger cage for a while, I was moved to an even larger cage where the vet lived. That was even better. I learned that the vet's wife's name was Carolyn. I had trouble pronouncing her name, so I called her Carol. There were two kids as well. Ken was the boy, and Nancy was the girl. There was also a dog named Casey and a cat named Muffin. The cat was black like me, but we didn't get along at first because she liked to chase birds. There were also some horses.

I enjoyed greeting whoever came to feed me. They would talk to me; and over time, I began to understand what they were saying. They would sometimes bring me treats that I would eat out of their hand, and they would stroke my back and pet me on the head. It wasn't long until they would come into the cage and call my name and hold out their arm for me to land on while I ate my treat.

Sometimes I would call Casey. He would come to the cage, and I would chat with him. I tried calling the cat, but she paid no attention to me. I really enjoyed having someone come and talk to me even if they didn't bring a treat. It was nice to have the company. I would ask, "How are you?" and they would answer and tell me about their day.

One day, I saw Ken and Doc closing all the barn doors. When Ken came into my cage, he called me to his arm and then held me while he walked to the barn door and went inside. There was hay and stalls, but all the horses were outside. I liked the horse and hay smell, and it was a bigger space than any of my cages. Ken set me on a stall gate, moved a short way down between the stalls, and called to me. I could see that he had one of my favorite treats. I flew to him and landed on his arm, and he told me what a good bird I was. Then he sat me on a gate again and said I could explore the barn all I wanted to. He threw a handful of corn (I love corn) down between the stalls and said, "Go eat it, Jocko." So that's what I did. Ken then sat in a chair by the door and watched while I explored the whole barn. It was really fun. When it was dinner time, Ken called me back to his arm, and I went back to my cage.

The next day, Ken and Nancy took me into the barn; and while Ken held me, Nancy showed me a big piece of hamburger (I love hamburger), let me smell it, and then walked down to the end of the barn and dropped it. Ken said, "Go find it." So I did!

The next time we did the same thing, but Ken didn't let me see where Nancy hid it. Then he said, "Go find it." It was a little harder this time, but I have a good sense of smell and great eyes. So I found it just fine. This became a really good game, and sometimes I would be hunting a piece of red cloth that I would bring back or a small toy. Then it was changed a bit, and Nancy would hide somewhere, and I would have to find her. That was fun also.

16

Of the horses on the ranch, I only liked two, and only two liked me. One was Molly, the prettiest horse of all. The other one was Tug. He was the biggest and oldest horse, and Doc called him retired. He wasn't ridden and didn't do any work anymore. I liked talking with Molly. I would sit on the fence, and we had some good talks. She warned me about one horse, but I forgot and landed on his stall gate. He reached for me with his teeth, and I barely escaped. I almost lost some tail feathers.

Summer was coming to an end. And one day, I heard Doc say to Carolyn, Ken, and Nancy, "It's time to let Jocko decide for himself if he wants to stay with us or go and be a wild raven." I heard them say they were afraid I would fly away and not come back, but Doc said it was the right thing to do.

So one sunny morning, Ken brought me out into the yard and set me on the fence. My cage was opened as were the barn doors, and the blue sky was there for me to explore again. I took off and soared high over the ranch and remembered how good it felt to just glide on the air currents. I had not flown much for quite a while, and I seemed to get tired soon. I headed back down to the ranch and had a warm and happy welcome back by everybody. Home felt good.

I flew more and more and tried to talk to some of the other ravens that were in the area. Most would not talk to me, and some tried to drive me away. I finally met one that would talk to me, and he said the other ravens were afraid of me because I could use human words, and they didn't trust me. I called him Jack, and he said that it would not be long before all the ravens and many other birds would start heading for warmer places before it snowed.

One very cloudy day, a man with a star on his coat stopped to talk to Doc. Ken said he was the sheriff and was getting people together to hunt for a missing little girl. Doc said they would all help and started to get in the truck. Ken called to me, and I landed on his arm as we got in the truck. Doc said, "Why are you bringing Jocko?" Ken explained that he heard the Sheriff say the clouds were too low for an airplane search, and he and Nancy had been playing hide-and-seek with Jocko for several months, and he had gotten pretty good at finding her and other things that they hid.

We got to a place where the family had been cutting wood, and they said they had left their daughter in the truck playing with her dolls and didn't check on her until they stopped to eat lunch. I heard them say she was five years old and had left the truck without her jacket. People began fanning out to search when Doc asked to let me smell her jacket; and then Ken said, "Go find her, Jocko." which is what he used to say when I would hunt Nancy. Sniffing the jacket helped. Ravens have a great nose for smells of all kinds. I started just hopping around to see which direction I should start looking. When I found a direction, I followed it in the air for a while and then flew above the trees. I couldn't go real high as the clouds were not far above the trees. So I flew back and forth, and it wasn't too long before I saw her sitting against a tree trunk sucking her thumb. I then flew as high as I could and called, "Here," as loud as I could. Pretty soon, some people came in my direction, and I flew down and hopped in front of them to the girl. Everybody was really happy!

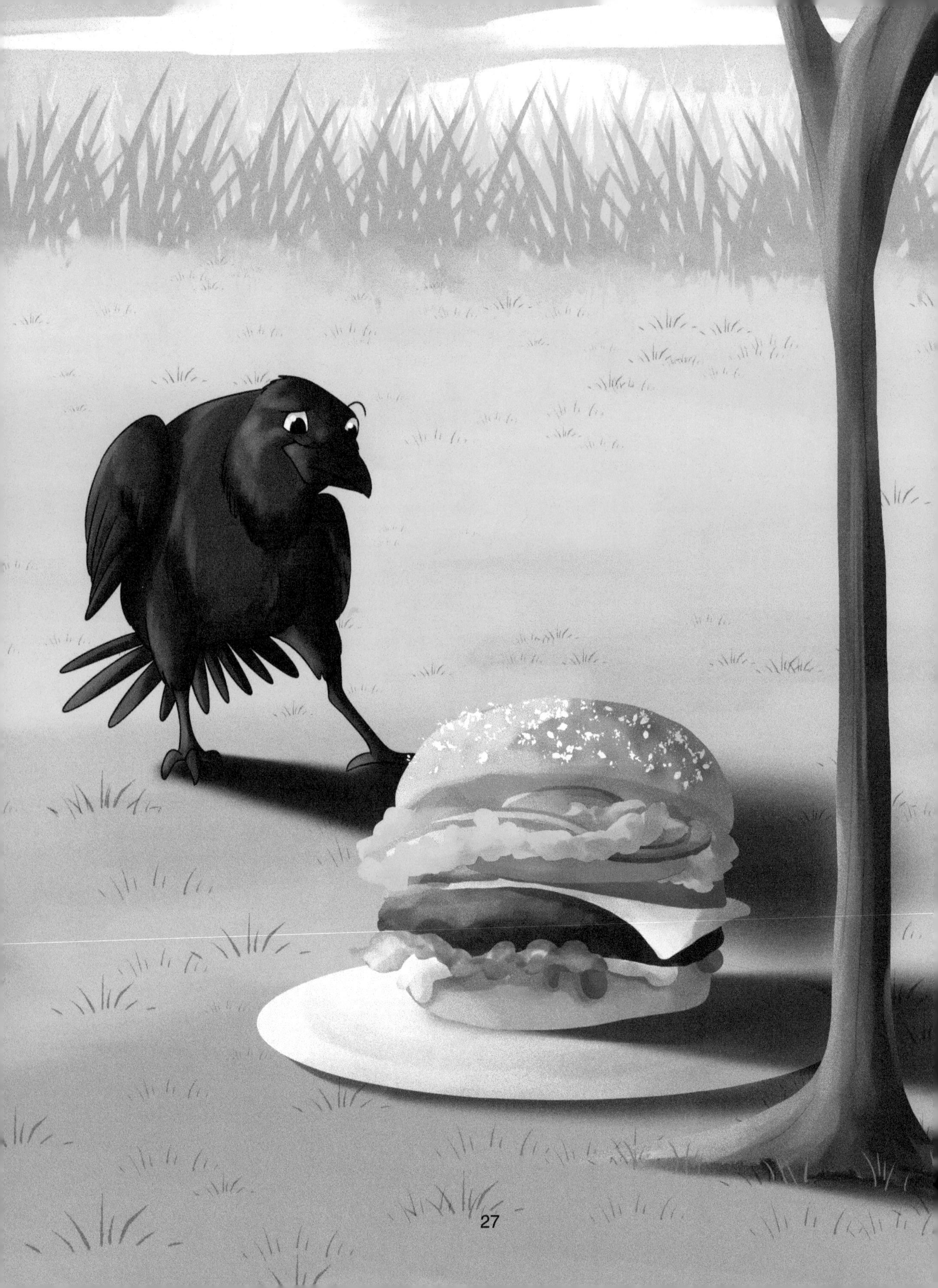

One day, I was gliding the air currents a little farther from the ranch than I usually fly, and I saw a huge hamburger on the edge of this field. It was as big as a plate with a bun, lettuce, tomato, and onion. I couldn't believe what I was seeing. It was just like Carolyn made for the family when Doc took the hamburger off the grill, only bigger. I was often fed some of everybody's hamburger. I had to check this out. I drifted down and began to hop over to it. That was funny. I couldn't smell anything. I thought I'll just check it out anyway. It really looked good. What could it hurt?

I went up to it and gave it a good peck and TWANG. I was lifted off the ground and found myself in a net. Oh, I was in trouble! It was quite a while before someone came. It was a man I had never seen before. I started to say something, but then I noticed his eyes and how happy he was to see me in that net. Birds and animals read and communicate with each other using the eyes and body language, and I didn't like this guy one bit. I decided to just keep quiet. He put the net in the back of the truck and drove to his house. We went into his barn; and when he reached into the net to get hold of me, I pecked him really hard. He yelped and pulled his hand back and got a small blanket to wrap around me. I was put in a cage, and he started talking to me, telling me to say something. He said, "I know you can talk. I heard you on a rescue that I was paid to go on. You're going to make me a lot of money as a talking bird. I'll be back later, and I'll make you talk if I have to." I was worried. If I didn't get back to the ranch, everyone would be worried. How do I get out of this mess?

After a while a cat came by and rubbed up against the cage and said, "Who are you?" I told her I just got caught and wanted to go home. She said, "What will you give me?"

I told her the cat at the ranch had a squeaky toy, and she was too old to play with it anymore. I would drop it off tomorrow. The cat said she had learned how to work the latch when she had been locked up once before. I said, "Do it." She did, and I was free in the barn. I just had to wait for the man to open the door, and I would be ready to fly out.

When the barn door opened, I flew out, and the man did a lot of yelling and jumping up and down. The next day, I dropped the toy in front of the cat. She was happy.

I was a lot more careful after that about checking things that didn't seem right.

When snow came, I spent more time in the barn, and my favorite place to sit or even sleep was on Tug's back. It was wide and warm, and he didn't mind a bit.

The days had gotten warmer, the snow was melting, and it was more fun to be outside flying over the country. One day, as I flew over the ranch, I saw Molly lying down in the grass. I flew down to see her; and when I landed in front of her she said, "Get Doc." So I flew back to the house and started calling "Molly" as loud as I could. Carolyn heard me, and I kept saying, "Molly," and hopping back toward the pasture.

Carolyn went in the house; and pretty soon, Doc showed up. He grabbed a jug of water and his bag and followed me, hopping toward the pasture. When we got there, Molly was glad to see him; and right away, he started helping Molly's new baby horse into the world.

As the weather warmed, Doc got another call from the sheriff that a small boy had wandered off from his parents' camp. Doc took me to the area, and it wasn't long before I found him. But a couple of coyotes had found him too. I wasn't sure what to do, but I had heard that coyotes weren't real brave. So I dove down in front of the boy and spread my wings as far as I could and said "Get out" as loud as I could. They didn't like that and took off at a run. Then I flew up over the boy and called "Here" as loud as I could until someone showed up.

After school and on some weekends, Ken and Nancy would play more search games with me. They would show me a small toy or ball and hide one like it for me to find. One time, Carolyn lost a ring in the garden when she took off her gloves. She showed me another ring and told me to find hers. It took me a while because it was small. But the ring was shiny, and I finally found it.

One time, I saw a young raven land in the corral with a hard biscuit in his beak. He began pecking it to try to break it up so he could eat it. I went over to him and said, "Let me show you something." I took the biscuit and flew to the water trough and dropped it in to soak. The young raven was really squawking at me to give it back, and he grabbed it out of the water and tried to peck it hard enough to break it up again. I took it back to the water telling him to just wait a bit, but he wouldn't listen and took it out and flew away.

‌∽

Jocko had many more adventures over the years and lived a long time.

TRUE STORY

Jocko was a real raven. Just like the story, he was shot and brought into my animal hospital. Everything in the story is just the way it happened. When it was time to turn him loose, I took him a few miles up Copper Basin and let him go. It wasn't long after that that Carolyn saw a raven sitting on the corral fence that didn't seem at all afraid of her. A few days later, a raven came and dropped a slice of dried bread in the water trough to soften it up. Over the next few years, he would repeat that process with dried biscuits or bread.

One time, he showed up with a biscuit in his mouth and a smaller companion. We assumed an offspring that he was going to teach how to soften it up. The youngster didn't want to wait and would grab it and hop down to eat it now. Of course, it was too hard to eat, and Jocko would pick it up and try again to soften it up. This was repeated a few times with the youngster squawking loudly the whole time. Jocko finally gave up and left the youngster to hammer away on the hard biscuit.

Ravens can learn to say words, but Jocko did not learn to talk while at the hospital.

About the Author

Dr. Ellsworth is a retired veterinarian and lives with his wife of sixty-two years in a mountain community in Central Arizona. He graduated with a degree in veterinary medicine from Colorado State University and served two years in the Army Veterinary Corps. He was then in mixed-animal practice in Arizona for the next thirty years. Dr. Ellsworth was a private pilot and used his plane to serve distant ranches. In his years of practice, he treated numerous injured ravens, horned owls, and a few hawks. Dr. Ellsworth coauthored *A History of Veterinary Medicine in Arizona 1887–1962.*

CPSIA information can be obtained
at www.ICGtesting.com
Printed in the USA
JSHW020814261219
3179JS00001B/1

9 781644 924754